Space Gulliver

PRAISE FOR SAMPURNA CHATTARJI'S POETRY

'Sampurna Chattarji's [poems] are tools of investigation into myth, history, metropolitan life and, importantly, the ambiguities of the personal quest for poetic expression... While some of Chattarji's poems can be expansive, encompassing cities, deserts, islands, the journeys of scholar-explorers and of migrating tribes, she can also produce poems that are spare, haiku-like in their compression, delicate and mysterious as netsuke.' – **Ranjit Hoskote**

'The poems in Sampurna Chattarji's *Absent Muses* dexterously balance the spirit of intellectual inquiry and dialogue with the impulse to emote. The poet's eye is well-trained, its gaze wide and its focus sharp and narrow, dwelling on the drama that inheres in small things. The voice is compelling, impossible to turn away from.' – **K. Srilata**, *The Hindu*

'Chattarji works within the radius of her intuition. Hers is a poetry of subtle impressions, far-off correspondences (but never far-fetched!), dissimilar images moulded into a poetic whole. She experiments fearlessly... Her poems can be disturbing. But in this day and age, what would a modern poet be worth if she can't upset the reader and shake him out of his equanimity?' – **Keki Daruwalla**

'In *Sight May Strike You Blind*...there is a new sense of entitlement - the freedom to extend the compass of one's subjects. There is a clear indication that the poetry is not going to be framed within traditional uncertainties. This brings in a sense of pleasure and playfulness - the ability to subject things to an intense but not necessarily self-involved gaze.' – **Anjum Hasan**, *Tehelka*

Space Gulliver

Chronicles of an Alien

Sampurna Chattarji

HarperCollins *Publishers* India

First published in India by
HarperCollins *Publishers* in 2015
Building 10, Tower A, 4th Floor, DLF Cyber City, Phase II,
Gurugram Haryana – 122002, India
www.harpercollins.co.in

This edition published in India in 2020 by HarperCollins *Publishers*

2 4 6 8 10 9 7 5 3 1

P-ISBN: 978-93-5357-606-6
E-ISBN: 978-93-5357-607-3

Typeset in 11/13 Goudy Old Style at
SURYA

Printed and bound at
MicroPrints India, New Delhi

for Kiran

Are they real? Is that a parking meter? A lamp post?
Is this what it means, to travel?

— Space Gulliver IV

When the aliens land they will take exactly that form that streak of silver cut with a sharp knife on a plate of blue a scratch by an elegant claw a beast you don't see because there isn't a beast the aliens are fine minute they travel at the head of a pin faster than the human eye can see you have to be a child lying back on a slope of grass or an adult on a reclining chair time-travelling into your past in order to see the path of their coming it is a moment of grace granted only to the chosen who know how to tilt the head back so you see the planet spinning the griffonlings on the wind the wish to be a painter in the simultaneity of things the depth and surface the smallest bird making the most effort little wings like clockwork springs whirring bare branches waving as the clouds pass and this is not about the weather but about the landings for there are more than one she sees each new coming with a breath of indrawn air a childish sound that startles her into delight, not one but another, another, each a thing of beauty and grace these etchings on the sky that mark the beginning, silver eyelashes left on the cheek of a blue god, pick up and make a wish remember to close your eyes and blow, she wishes them happy landing, how will they slow down once they enter our world these unerringly beautiful people who have travelled faster than the speed of sound and now they know she is watching and aren't reticent anymore they blaze comet trails behind them spectacular showy things the sun applauds with a burst of light and its fierceness stabs her through the eye she has to look down, look away, humbled, as if the sun were telling her: what really matters is what you cannot bear to look at, were saying: for some, breaking barriers is an intervention, cruel, artificial, but for me it is as simple as bursting through a cloud.

No cathedral more distracting than sky

Grass spongy

The sprung rhythm of feet

The hum of traffic

Binding solitary to passerby

This window open to all

Seen by none

The *we* of traffic

We: *hum* in Hindi

Country of origin: India

Green chilli, baby corn

Come closer to the tamped earth

Space Gulliver returns
Space conqueror, she
        Between too much space and too little
Lies a sky of infinitives
Split
That chest of carved and polished wood lies within her reach
But she will not touch it
She is a visitor now
And earthly things disturb her
Materialize
All around her with their unflinching edges their resolute past
Even the drapes on the walls
And the intricately carved bedspread on which she
Lies
Frighten her with their ornate proximity their embroidery
That speaks of pain
Staking its territory as needles stab fabric in a million hands
On the dresser with the clouded mirror is a picture of a boy
Outside the window is a maze of cut animals
Space Gulliver has become laughably used to living in
Boxes
Tubes
Cylinders
Gasmasks
Bodysuits
Shuttles
Laughably used to having Brahmand around her
As if all those light years were nothing but a warm
Woollen Himalayan blanket around her knees
She is no longer terrified of vastness
Her space eyes have taught her to see in the dark

The travelling centaurs the bursting casanovas
Heads of saints
Silver is now her favourite colour the unbearable silver of
The cold sun trying to tear the steel cloud which imprisons it
        every morning
Warm tones make her shiver breathe hectic
Swallowtones
Gulp swallow gulp swallow the fresh air that is rationed into
        the room
Earlier she might have died trying
To establish a perfect precise relationship between her
And every object in the room
        Ever since her return to earth
She has been sitting at the window
And reconciling herself

The cathedral appears only when dark
Falls
The cathedral has cognition
Knows when it will be upstaged
By day
It is a grey building
By night
It is glory alleluia
In a shimmy of stardust

Space Gulliver knows she is watched
She likes being watched by the great benignness
Just as she likes laughs that boom boyishly out of men
Known for their secret solemnity
        Do eyelashes grow back she wonders
She likes watching the great benignness back
Even though it makes her head spin
Now that she is no longer used to gravity's
Rainbow pinning her down
The sky is still only when you're moving below it
Oblivious as anthills hiding storytellers
        If you sit still and watch as Space Gulliver does
You see it moves
        The entire sky taking us along
The edge is a good place to sit when you wish
To regard the world you had insanely loved
And now feel only a puzzled affection for
Space Gulliver hates the personal pronoun
Prefers hares that bound across the road
Prefers ravens large as horses
Magpies that know crime in black and white
Prefers staring
        The notion of a page is false
If measured in screen space
How do you know where the line ends?
Space Gulliver unbridles her horse
Escapes on the bare back of the runaway sentence
Someone close the door of the barn

Monsters may do what men may not. In your country what is a monster? In mine, there are many demons, some hideous, but none beastly, none monstrous in the way you mean, just god becoming man becoming beast becoming god. Overnight a hole appears in the wall, as if Narasimha has climbed out of her story earlier that evening and not finding a pillar to break out of chosen instead a plain white plaster wall next to the lift and the fire extinguisher. Who among the roistering lads did he come to save from a monstrous father? Which of them in hoods and sneakers was glad to be delivered from rex tyrannicus, demon-king, doer of terrible penances, capable of standing on one foot for millennia, shaming the son who has a religious streak, turned vegan, reads poetry? Poetry is not plastic surgery, said the poet in her hometown, before she left. The limits of individual plasticity, said the lecturer in the seminar room, after she arrived. Is there a point beyond which the individual hardens into the concrete unchangeable? Is that you, age four and you, age fourteen and you, age forty-one? You've changed, but it's you all right. The only god is writing, the poet wrote in her book, before she left. Yes, but what of the god in disguise, the god who assumes half-human half-animal form to tear out the guts of a father before his only son's eyes? Feed him gratitude, stupor him into drinking, slowly, the milk meant for a newborn calf.

Puss in fur boots
Morning strides off
Looking for exit routes
Conifers confer
Agree that concealment is the best
Defence
Morning is not amused
When she discovers
Thirsty-Light
Is really
Thirty-Eight
A number on a door
Such possibilities
Missed!
Reality is mud
Lining every crack
Under her soul

Space Gulliver's new walking shoes are purple
As if enchanted, she hasn't stopped longing to walk
Ever since she tried them on in the store of a thousand boots
Where the furred tongues were wagging soft courtesies
To her toes
Seven league boots
One giant leap
Vamana the dwarf
She could possess everything with three small steps
Earth heaven the headless horseman
Blue Velvet venison sausages and Shrove Tuesday
You've left it too late, the pencilled secretary tells her,
It's Commodity Monday
The date marked in red is 271
Space Gulliver is still getting used to getting time in little boxes
Which she must fill with her attention
Instead she longs to walk, leave the window, enter the woods
Follow the sun as it teases its path through her head
Twigs snap their fingers at her purple boots
Leaves scurry obeisance
Winds wish her godspeed whirling her away with the rain
Her pennant is an umbrella turned inside out
        When the young people walk by in their glittering skins
And flyaway hair, Space Gulliver retreats to her shelf
Hides in a bowl of tiny sweet oranges

The A74 in Glasgow is closed delays of up to an hour London underground trains have severe delays classic fm it's seven-thirty this bubble of sound never bursts blowing from the lips of singers with enough breath to compete with a whale a vast blowhole of exultation singling its way into the hesitations between curves and straights, roads where you will brush against the sharp points of the Munich Symphony Orchestra the flower duet crocus and snowdrop horses in red blankets whinny in St Petersburg the bridges open at two Olga learns ballet in town will make pancakes tomorrow it's Pancake Tuesday hot cross buns fill the room with cinnamon sound poems spring out of biography like the first flowers that suggest a thawing she dreams of hands local honey fierce cows speed cameras under her pillow she folds the next morning a talisman avoids looking into the rooms of people she barely knows tapes posters to fridge doors photographs her meals waltzes into the circularity of dining rooms where daffodils bloom on stalks of bright and edible green not only will we have a stronger border in future it will smell like plums sound like marbles in a very white mouth

In town the cathedral is everywhere
Around corners
Dodging Cinderella
Franciscan priory
Monkseye
Piece of Wall
Breathing down
Every street
Moroccan
Glasseyed
Stores
What links
Street to street
But this
Medieval presence

The most persistent memory is bird-call. Helicopters skim the horizon summoning the men in fluorescent green, talking machines in their hands, at the perimeter a balding man stands waving everyone away, accident is a mystery but through the darkling branches she sees another green fluorescence guarding the road from something that has not yet been uttered. 'Five hours' floats up and that is all, the field dims, a single shaft lights up the whole universe which is here out on the grass shorts books cans of cola cigarettes and cameras players erupt Frisbees slice the air dudes in sunglasses punch their Macs into music elegant black girls reveal the beauty of their smiles tents spring up sound carries farther on such a day his back to a tree a little man reads his book with admirable detachment from the festal fields around him drought in the south ban on hosepipes and showers how long will the bald and burly man wait at the border of unnameable punching his silver gadget, tying his laces? Gold lamé is a gesture that bridges the morning and night, no idyll uninflected by tragedy so this serene summer evening hotter than Algeria bruised without her knowing, her small worries of a crick in the back a catch in the throat a chill in the chest when outside her window between St Giles and Downs a girl has died hit by a car while crossing the road all evening sirens sing ceaselessly accidents accumulate between junctions two and one classic fm it's five-thirty why does everyone sit facing the sun?

Space Gulliver has never seen a gull before
The reason why Space Gulliver thinks
She has never seen a gull before
Is that her memories of gulls are linked to water
This far inland she looks at the great white birds coasting
Outside her window and is filled with first-time-ness
Sometimes when she doesn't see but hears
A harsh shriek it reminds her of the gull's shape its clean wings
Cruel beak but recent memory is all she relates it to
This far from water aren't the birds homesick for the sea
Perhaps it appears far to her who has abandoned the great
machines
That lent her speed and cannot travel anymore as the crow
flies
For her to measure where she is how far from where she was
She will need instruments that torture
Needles that point dials that encompass gauges that fill
With secrets she is saving for the time she will read her own
memoir
Where the lost memories were
There now sit fantastic inventions
A palace in Versailles she lived in
A zeppelin she flew
A shaman she loved with
Mustard flowers growing on walls

On this very day
In 1723
Handel was appointed
As Royal Composer
But he couldn't get paid because
As the document says
He was an alien.
Did he arrive then playing a blue streak
Landing on the square
Before the cathedral
With a small surprising jolt?

Space Gulliver finds her sister: the ladybird
Neither lady nor bird it sits on the thick glass window
A hemisphere unto itself
It has travelled a long way to see her
From thirty-five years ago
It has ridden on the blade of sharp green grass
That cut the tongue if you sucked it
That hid four-leaf clovers and the fallen mysteries of moth
To arrive, unannounced, as only a relative may
Here on the thick glass window
That measures four degrees to her bare palm
As she rests it next to the ladybird in a gesture
Of simple recognition
That her sister misunderstands as violence
Wings springing out of its body
Like the blades of a flick knife
Ladybird tumbles and lies on her back on the sill
Tumbling as she does from *it* to *she* seamlessly
Space Gulliver tries to help her find her balance
And succeeds
Heedless and somewhat cunning Ladybird sits
Absolutely still
Playing dead
Space Gulliver takes a photo of her sister
For the family album
So small she has to hold the camera
Close, so close focus blurs
And all she gets is a little black dot
When she turns back to the window
Ladybird has flown
Such slyness!
Putting her camera away

Space Gulliver puts the question to both of them
Herself and runaway kin:
How far must they fly to really get away
How useless are those little wings
Is this the one she loved
Twelve thousand seven hundred odd mornings ago
Stomach crushed against the wet green on a hillside
Her breath the only cloud?

At midnight
The cathedral
Disappears

Space Gulliver adores this vanishing
How whimsical the sky is when you're below it
Instead of in it
Its intrusiveness
As it leans down to smother you in a cloud of breath
Saying hah
Now see if you can find your way through the thicket
She knows why the lamp post has returned
Why lamp posts are necessary
In this landscape that would be nothing without
The sky
        The lion was a symbol
She read him purely as lion and loved him
His voice his mane his strength which he knew
How to curb
So his great paw could be light as a caress
        The witch was real
Complicated only by her ignorance of snow
Which she had seen fall
Once
But disallowed play so the softness of it
The coldness of it were no more than signs
Seen in a dream
The only thing she didn't need to touch or eat
To know as real
Was the whiteness of it
Verifiable by eyes alone
By the dazzling scar it left
Inside where images are reversed
Into meaning
The queen the carriage the blandishments

The wolves
All, all understood
        The wardrobe was functional
Changing function with the lack of befuddlement
Only enchantment allows
Bathtub: a place to have baths
        Altered
Bathtub: a place to float boats
Such transformations needed boys, brothers
Needed metal and candle and fire
Because these were no ordinary boats
And falling headlong into the tub full of water
Would not take you away to the sea
Full of armadas and flotillas and battleships
And pirates
You had to *engineer* its happening
And in that word Space Gulliver always
Imagined
A sneer
A curling of the lip that warned against escaping
Lightly
Mocked the flimsiness of paper
The deludedness of lions witches and wardrobes
The absurdity of lamp posts
Lit in the day so that when the mist came
And the world vanished
One little girl could still advance fearlessly
Towards another world
Fictitious
And so
        Believable

Sabotage the Hot Sausage Co. that needs a trailer to come and drive it away when the street is lifted from bustle into the gloaming call of cafés Calgary is here inside the church no one visits St Augustine in mosaic raises his shepherd's crook the temptation to adopt a plant is overwhelmingly unpractical even though in the room a clean white ceramic bowl awaits just such a guest far from the bells that signal the service has begun it's nice to have the sun *no it isn't* just a boy being cheeky and when the clean bright feeling is over another replaces it warm and welcome a small raw patch of skin on the finger he has bitten close to the nail handing her a plastic glass of red wine in the upper upper stalls closest to the gods knees press against the hard railing that will save them from tumbling down opposite in the little boxes couples backlit like marionettes the spectacle is everywhere she wishes for flies' eyes a hundred to accommodate each pair of arms each shock of hair each bending into instruments of wood and string such a soft plucking can lead to this dense thicket of sound string become percussion the deep red call of flesh only when she shuts her eyes can she hear the small woman with the elfin face who loves her violin differently from the woman with the muscled bare arms who wears a skirt and keeps her legs apart her face rising to the hand that calls her and her of the pale breasts shown simply without display in a plunging v-neck dress that sheathes her like a mermaid's skin tail flaring where her feet should have been small sad drooping breasts she answers with her flute suddenly her body animated as it arches towards the man who holds them all young fluid blond hands that draw her out and her of the curly locks and slender tenor saxophone all these women blowing into their pipes swooping onto their strings lip and mouth and shoulder and thigh and chin at once stable and liquid moving everywhere impossible to look just at him or her or him and her this is what the Russian fairytale would sound like if it were turned into notes obsessed with death and pleasure a giant orgasm orchestrated by the faun with the golden hair whose fingers make them fall upon their bows suddenly savage except her of the big bass drum who feels no need to quiver and places each thumping beat squarely into the centre of her own unregarded self

Space Gulliver prefers the complicity of the horizon
In this enterprise called 'seeing'
She is used to the fact that devices need to be paired
Before they can speak to each other
Before this act so close to intercourse can take place
Him entering her phone directly
When it fails
Device not discoverable
Space Gulliver starts into guilt
        Even here
        In amoral tech heaven
There is an abstract entity sensing sin censoring desire
Construing adultery in the simplest swap
His fingers on her keys
        To her who has lived without human contact for aeons
Stretching her fingers apart to see him better
Feels like the most intimate contact
As if she has really touched his hair
His neck his waist
Instead of merely the soft skin
Of the device that nestles at his hip
Or at his ear
Accepting his mouth
Just as her straining eyes must accept that
On some days
The mid-morning moon that strikes her with its
Deranged light
Is really the sun
And the mid-afternoon half-moon in a sky of no dimension
Is really the moon
And that the horizon is capable of receding
The way her body recedes

After half a bottle of red
Into a farness comforting in its extremity
Like the words she has been reading all night
Oscillating magicians and mathematicians
Demanding no understanding
But the kind that passes directly into the blood
Temporariness temporariness
The tempo of the chronically aware
For whom a girl with one white stocking and one black
Is not the day slowing down
But rather the trees shredding shadows
Into the sweetest illusions

Feels like four degrees
Quickly treat your
Extremities
To heat
Light the small glow
In the centre of your chest
Recall the axe
The lowered head
In the stained
Glass window
Pigeons gurgle
Lasciviously
Bringing the sound
Of Bombay
Into the room

Space Gulliver is competing with the light
Who will dazzle the roomful of pigeons more?
Glaucous is the word
That enters her eye like a mote
She blinks too often, the lens inside needs
Changing again
Out there, a place she is now remembering
With longing instead of dread
Out There she saw through instruments fitted
To the eye like clocks
Bulbous, bug-like, she had been able to out-stare
The Light
But in the room full of soft plump pigeons
            Their plumed breasts
            Their feathery necks
            From which they will slowly unwind
            Scarf ribbon shawl
            Shed cloak cape coat
            A simultaneous moulting that terrifies her
Space Gulliver can no longer bear
The sharp light that enters mercilessly
She cannot turn away, the angle of the room
Does not permit it
She needs to summon the help of her body
It is instinct, any of the pigeons in the room
Could do it without blinking a red eye-lid
But Space Gulliver has never studied that word
'Instinct'
Half her face is pulsing with this heat heavy as a sheet
Of glass
Half her body
If she swivels, all of her will be thugged by the light

If she excuses herself and retires to her room
Up the narrow stairs to weep in frustration
Even there the light has gouged mirrors on the walls
If she does this inexcusable thing
She will not escape
Her incomprehension of the body
She forgot when she climbed aboard
And went as far as the machine could take her
        'Sexless'
Inexact
        'Unsexed'
Space Gulliver feels muffled giggles exploding inside her
Like damp patakas
Pigeons in heat
        'Why is this room so hot?'
        'Because I come from a tropical country.'
Space Gulliver has always wanted to say that
Knowing saying will make it true
Meanwhile, the pigeons flutter in impatience
Stare at her
Expecting instruction, enlightenment
Space Gulliver would love to set a cat among them
A lean young thing
Feral in a coat that clings to it unsheddable
Remote and lethal
A panther
She needs a cub in the room
A small black danger
        This is a new failing
        This capacity for distraction
Muddled, Space Gulliver stands there
And it is clear

If she stands long enough
The pigeons will leave
The light will shift its searing brilliance
Away from the nape of her neck
The white of her eye
The floor that it glints into an unbearable sea
And she will be able to walk towards
Her silhouette
A small black shape
Growing larger as she enters it

Choose your hair carefully the burgundy coat may be outmoded by summer and what will you do then with your synchronized burgundy hair? There must be a reason some people always choose the seats hugging the walls and others the seats furthest from the windows. Advertisements for college presidents walk past waving arms and legs mouths moving in soundless animation the dominant colour is poster-blue the blue-haired girl limps past twice punctuating purple pink white multi-coloured, did I mention blue? Is touching allowed? A grey-haired man with his back to the room touches the blushing girl on the arm above the elbow. 'No it's about history.' The leap of her heart shocks her so much she ignores the boy completely, drinks her chocolate, chocolatl, Aztec, mighty ruins, tremendous poems. This is what happens when you only know one face in a sea of faces like the lone word you can read in a sea of foreign print. He doesn't see her and when he walks through the window and away, she is viscera: gut: entrail: divination: omen: bird: skin: disease: welt: world. Erotic charge hidden in her poems, avoidance of closure, tools of investigation, guardedness. The pattern of his sweater returns on the back of a Japanese boy, hordes of Japanese boys, sneezing violently.

Space Gulliver has fallen in love
The ultra-shine quality in magic quantum
Is what she has fallen in love with
        Disquisition, she feels like telling someone
        Tugging at their sleeve
        That's the word I've fallen in love with
Is that an ocelot or an aye-aye?
Is that an anoa?
Genet, you old world carnivore!
Goanna, you lizard
        Space Gulliver is experiencing delirium
Like the weightlessness she was once
Addicted to
It is only at the beginning of falling
That you experience delirium
She tells herself
With the sternness of the auto-didact
        When the ultra-shine quality of magic quantum
Illuminates the mass that is moving towards you
At the speed of light of thunder
Of fallen lightning
That's when space vanishes
He might have been wearing her seven-leaguers
The way his strides swallowed the earth the sky the gulf
Between them
Which an instant ago was solid, carpeted
Held down by human- and table-legs
Chairs holding bodies
Not astral not remotely luminous
Until this happened
The magic shine of ultra-quantum

Hyperbolic parabola
The path you took towards me
Never reduce me to me again
Space Gulliver chastises him
With a joy
She might have considered unbecoming in someone
Of her age
And gravity
If it weren't for curve points equidistance
Wonders that make her shine
Like the quality of magic
This quantum ultravenously
Surrounding her with its smell of sky
        This is heaven, then
Space Gulliver thinks, as she wears his scent
Left lightly on her breast
And moves through the minutes
At a very secret gallop
        This disappearance of place
An elephant on one finger a serpent around the other
In this paradise the serpent is beautiful
Wise as the elephant is strong
In this space beyond space which is heaven
Each animal sounds like its name
So you can recognize it
Though you have never seen it before
The colocolo a South American wild cat, the komondor a
        Hungarian dog
The book at your doorstep in the middle of the night
In the middle of your rumpled room
A Manual of Tibetan Grammar

The xenopus an African frog, the bulbul a Persian bird
Tahr your wildness your long torso your short stout recurving
hands
Tamarin your silky hair
If all these names exist, then why not love?

When open
Curtains
Reveal
Not the city
Lit-up
Like a girl
In love
But an absolute
Blackness
You
Think
Someone has
Finally
Put out
Your
Heart

The pharaoh will save us, goats, livers, cheese. In a goods shed by the railway tracks candelabras dance across the walls, the feeding is sumptuous, fresh, the heart can be reached only by sawing the breastbone, her eyes are ravaged, except when she is listening with her palm against her cheek, two lovely black eyes, there was a birthmark she surrendered to the surgeon's knife, gothic houses come true as she speaks, perhaps only three women could speak this way, spindle scissor thread, rock paper scissor, tearing muscle from shell with swift small fingers, choosing orange and pear, drawing comfort from a whiskey bottle kept in a drawer in a room smelling of the one who lived in it before. Every story demands listening with hands, mouth, back, shoulders, at the end of this conversation she will return with a pain all over, as if she exercised parts she never uses anymore. Every face looks medieval in this light, chiaroscuro, this flattering flame. Beams and rafters, potatoes, sea salt, shelves holding bottles like genies, this morning the sky was a lid pressing down, what should she do with this extra day, what has she ever done except splinter razor head?

Space Gulliver is expecting the Dalmatian to appear at the window
It is not unusual to expect Dalmatians at windows on days this sunny
On grass this green
It would in fact be a lot more unusual if it didn't appear, its body
Arching to receive the ball in its mouth
A silly happy giddiness in its gait
Windows yield what you want to see
It is a kindness, Space Gulliver believes
Carving up scenes into sections
That can be looked at, part by part
Like repeating I love you I love you
In square or rectangular fragments
So that when you're looking at the Dalmatian
You can see that love is a dog
When you're looking at the ball thrown by the arm
That the window does not reveal
You can see that love is that unrevealed arm and
What it is about to throw
When you're looking at the grass below the Dalmatian's paws
You see that love is capable of growing
When you're looking at the shadow cast by the dog
On the grass as the ball leaps towards his mouth
You see that love is a series of movements
When you look at the shadow below the Dalmatian
So narrow and so dark

You see that love is so narrow and so dark
        When a scrap of bird appears it is different, of course
The level changes, the sky widens
And it is the beginning
That marks impatience

No concatenation of letters
Too simple
A triangle
Of doors
B
F G
Behind them
Bahrain
Russia
India
Not to mention
Norway
And who knows
What other land
On the other side
Of the hyphen
That links these three
Others
Moroccan tomatoes
Rice from Pakistan
Spanish aubergines
The BFG
Would have loped past

Our windows
Grinning wildly
Bottling our dreams
Sp[r]outing
In[cr]edible
Words

Marked with a blue cross the sofa the mug the radio the window items on sale the reflection in the window the legs on the sofa the lips on the mug the voice on the radio marked with a blue cross more fun less money dressed as a Spanish lady with my fan and a flower in my hair price includes parts labour and safety checks your local blood bank is running low self esteem running low her hair so glossy even in this resolution her cheek so taut her sari so resplendent leaning forward this is perfection and when you talk like that the men go mad redemption is not seeing images of others intact in their beauty thirty five thousand pounds a number worth hanging on to as the blue cross travels marking chocolate truffles frying pans finding a way in the dark wrists weak with wringing a name like Hummerstone may be worth adopting if only to inscribe on a small white card a small blue cross that is the opposite of 'I understand everything' isolation like a hair-shirt worn willingly the abject d'art

Space Gulliver's idea of return is qualified by the notion
of pink
The pinkness gathering along the edges of the sky like a
ruched skirt
The sweetening of milky white gulls by a rose tincture
Candy light as the wind tosses them above roofs that are
linked in brownness
A café on a rooftop may not be a whimsical dream
But useful
A place for humans to find the warmth that is apportioned
whimsically
By day and tubular rooms by night
Like the stalks of leeches
Composition involves
Mug: yellow, vase: glass, flowers: preferably yellow and wide
open
Though slightly drooping
As if the day has weighed heavy on them too
Chair, window
Outside: approached from the sealed reticence of inside
'Outside' the first word that a baby might learn to say instead
of all the others
In this composition constancy is valued
Experiment frowned upon
This is a slow conventional set piece in which,
Space Gulliver thinks, wryly,
In which likeness has to do with warm glow rather than
resemblance
The ness added to any word warping it towards similitude
Drabness, for example, the drabness of brown bricks as the
pink leaks

Into the watery grey
Preceding night
Bridge, Space Gulliver thinks, why bridge when they mean weakness
Why not funicular, meaning ascending, the return of an angel?

Man sitting on fence not a metaphor anymore but a lonely figure of doubt black on a very green field a very brown fence constructed of wooden sticks or perhaps logs the small figure of man a boy really perched on it like an otter in the midst of nowhere sun on his face he doesn't feel the wind as don't the passengers in the sealed car the aquiline profile reflected in a patch of sky the sign that says only 243 miles to Glasgow is Rhyl *rill* is Flint *stone* or *skin* is that sea or land that has lost itself or marsh that is just beginning to swell are those two old people walking their dog along Colwyn Bay happy are their ears not cold is that girl sitting opposite from Somalia her lips are lush she is into Aeneas is the man at the snack bar Jamaican who are these people like birds even gulls lose their balance in such a high wind they teeter and tumble outside the safety of the room which loses socks and monkeys that are littler than she imagined where do the long boats go down these narrow rivers a salad is a fine cake she wrote in tender buttons truck horns are dragons on a windy hilltop radiators need diagrams to be understood by one from a tropical country when she saw the big wrecked ship rusting slowly in a field of new green gasp was not what escaped her but rather that the same phenomenon repeats itself until it slowly attains intelligibility just as jumping into the wrong coach is inevitable and the kindness of strangers a Welshman a Maltese woman and a drive through consonants that ease into the script of love following the yellow cup from seashells to dresser to table to bed

Space Gulliver adrift
That was how they made them in the movies
Bodies like bubbles
            They rarely mentioned metal
The thing that saved you
The sheets you had to rip through if you
Wanted to touch someone from a dream
Bloodying yourself all over
Mirrors were always convex on that ship
And disrepair a condition of comfort
Huge fronds of weed
Sea that spoke
Every cauldron bubbling with tomorrow
            Transport
            Yourself
Isn't that what they taught you in the schools
Where fabric was an essential lie
To move from one place of prayer to another
So wearying
The shards of habit
If she had stayed
The bright steel anchor through her heart
Like a hooked fish
The waterfront would have drunk her health
The rowers would have carried her high upon their shoulders
The walking dogs and running women
Would have sniffed and swallowed her
The blue tables on the pier would have sat her down
In a spot exactly proportioned between sun and shade
And offered her the meat of the lamb
Above her a persistent sound would have tugged her

Head in its direction
The small circling vision of a plane
That might yet dive right into a little boy's
Hands
Propellers transport her
And then she sees they have all rusted
Scrapped and refigured into thrones made entirely
Of the detritus of war
And yet how beautiful the identifiable pieces
Of bullet gun grenade pin bullet cartridge belt bullet
Holster handle speedometer coil mask propeller
Responsibility
Who is responsible for such macabre beauty that
One can buy
Sit on
Hang on a wall
And weep over
Space Gulliver's love mangled into these shapes
The propeller moves her
And one false step with her head in the clouds
Would have propelled her freezing into the
Place
Where cliffs rose and fell
Bearing people who had forgotten how to breathe
And still hadn't died
So used to suffocation fresh air unnerved them
Spasmed their cheeks
Pressured their ears
Into drums that beat with the fierce
Warning they ignored
        Plumed horses trot through a park
Spears and helmets lance the sun

Space Gulliver stays close to the ground
Allowing metal bars hinges doors and people
To obstruct her from every view that might
Remind her of the futility of moving
To and fro
A lullaby blown to pieces by
An insistent fire alarm
            If every warning can be ignored
When will true peril come
When the sharp provocation back to earth
Alarm bells will never be metaphorical again
They have taught her one thing
How to be ready to flee
All her essentials packed in a very small bag
A change of clothes
A pouch of medicines
Socks
Specs
Soap
A bar of something chewy
Something sweet
A bottle of water
This is all that would matter
In the end

And then the sun passes through clouds like a Viking
ship a shining that moves from sea to sea eclipsing the grass
rubbing the bulrushes into the kind of golden fur that
exists in dreams of children running across a field much
larger than this looking a kind of listening to the wind

Space Gulliver's new posture of resistance:
Left hand fisted in her pocket while right hand holds an apple
Delicious and crunchy as the sunlight
She is biting into
She was until seconds ago unaware of it as resistance
Or posture
Or even new
But something about the cheeping and trilling and whistling
All around her
Alerts her to the possibility of posture
Makes her happy because resistance needn't always be
Aggressive
Forgive the hard clenched bones of fist
Reminds her that to recognize what is new
Is like singing
Heavy roar of vehicles
Radio music from sports car
Zippiness of morning
Even grinning with one's mouth wide open need not
Feel like the thing only a finger-puppet might do
She is always holding something tight
It took the morning and the apple to tell her so

Trying to describe a man as a slender blue bolt or a foal or a colt as he enters the room like a spark igniting is impossible. Days like holes in a wedge of cheese like curtains drawn against a night so blue it runs onto the page like cobalt he is sudden and so the heart has no time to prepare itself and the shells on the windowsill are filled. Near the river where the air is icy she kneels in mud breathes hard feels her heat roaring these are oaks these are ash those are sheep those are lambs gambolling this is my house. No recollection of how they crossed the room from chair to door to arms like crossing oceans in two nimble steps. The slant of his body like a ray of lightning angling and falling just where the darkness is heaviest. The dodo had a very heavy heart. It could not run. It did not taste good. It died. The man like a bolt from the blue transformed into a way of holding so light she is untethered by all but him. Trying to describe his lips on her neck a quick soft brushing certain small but definite kiss like the conclusion of a thought begun a long time ago is impossible. They cannot cling to each other but perfume knows no such law. He leaves his sweet fresh scent on her. This has never happened before and will not happen again. When he leaves the day will drown around them and with no one watching, their leavetaking will be heavy, no quick steps away, mist entering the room, every word becoming harder to drag to her lips, sludge, slug, her head light with vanishing, slower and slower each moment like a breath she cannot take, he is leaving, taking the quickness with him and her tongue is tied and then suddenly all of her filled with a galloping haste go away go away so I can breathe again speak again to the trees, the walls, the windowpane.

Space Gulliver's sadness is monumental
Monumental her desire for friends
Who will draw her back into joy
Poets who will write songs for her
Poets she will write poems for
Poets who will offer her room in their small
One-room flats
Poets who will understand that flatness of emotion is not the
thing
Poets who write in languages she cannot read
Poets who vanish so swiftly she must have dreamed them up
Poets who tower above her
Or stand easily beside her shoulder to shoulder at a bar
Poets she could smoke with in a fine drizzle
Poets she could smoke with under lamp posts sizzling with
moths
Poets she could be loud with like sixteen years of carousing
And no knowledge it ends in death
Poets in slippers and shorts
Poets who once had stammers
Poets with preposterous and ironic eyebrows
Who will hold her as she stands in the sea
Poets who eat only raw food and watch the light fade
Poets so beautiful they lose everything
Poets with orange notebooks filled with sketches
Poets with cardamom on their tongues
Poets let loose in a country house
Poets reading
Sitting in large carved chairs wearing their glares
In the middle of the night

Poets who can walk into bedrooms unembarrassed by shed
skins
And the detritus of thinking oneself unobserved
Poets who have chased monkeys
And saved red books with golden letters from destruction
Poets with footballer's hands
Poets who buy her rings
Poets who buy her drinks
Poets who teach her words she may never need to use
Poets who have vertigo
Poets who once lived in brothels
Poets who have children from many women
Poets who build their own houses then leave them for sheds
in the garden
Poets who hold her hand
Poets with very soft lips
Poets singing suddenly
Haunting her long after
Poets on the floor sitting cross-legged with the door ajar
And the windows blowing
Eating with their fingers which they have never done before
Poets rambling falling quiet wanting to cry
Poets catching buses and trains to see her
Poets leaving in small blue cars
Poets driving lime-green Citroëns with sun-roofs left open
So wind chills ears and everyone wears a cap
Poets careful not to trample on moss
Walking through Blair Witch forests
Linking arms but not too close
For fear of misunderstandings
Poets in jackets that make a swishing sound
Poets born in Ethiopia

Poets hugging poets
Poets writing in pink ink on the title pages of their books
Poets making promises
Riding motor-bikes
Poets being asked to leave it's closing time
Poets in blue sweaters that cling
Poets in boa constrictors
Poets forgetting their lines
And what it was they were meant to do
Poets momentarily lost
Poets posing
Taking photos, always the same photos
Poets kissing her on the mouth
        Why does it have to be a poet?
Space Gulliver thinks
        Why not
Parachutist or pediatrician
Poltergeist or puppeteer
Pickle-maker or punk
        Because
Poets know
Know crows and alphabets
Know Fibonacci numbers and Gypsum Red D
Know anti-poem and counterpoint
Know tree and reed
Know *there was nothing inside*
Know Beelzebub in Bombay
Know canticles and Karna
Know wanting to be a roof is not a sign of insanity but of love
Know kindness is everything
Know the eerie longing
Know pelvises and shoulders

Know old houses where men hung themselves
Know beds in Peru
Know figurines the shape of Amsterdam
Know linguine and lascivious
Know
Philharmonic
Oysters, hieroglyphics and axes
Know girls from A to Z
Know one-camel clans and Babylon
Know lost earrings in grass
Know spectres in glass
Know the basket-weaver's love
Know how
To remain alone at the end of a rhyme that will not deceive you
Know cliffs
And the circus animals' desertion
The rag and bone shop of the heart
Know long grey beard and glittering eye
Know salt and sea and synaesthesia
Know horizon
Where she came from
Knowing nothing but the daft unsolvable
Equation

Turn off the sound so you can hear the whales.

Space Gulliver in her lost socks
You don't need bees, you need air
Seamless continuity from bitter to
Too sweet
Fixed to fluid
Random the house of the heart
Book of African proverbs never read
Productive
Hibernation
Always someone to latch on to
Bolt in a door
Bitemarks on skin
Breast of chicken
Leg of lamb
Heart of stone
This is a race of eaters
And makers of phrases that deny
The way the light stung
        Where, Space Gulliver wants to ask,
Are those elephants?
What are these connections
With colanders and hot towels?
When does the slicing of mushrooms
Turn into a disavowal
The sound of running
Water
A roar
That excludes humans?

This bathroom is alarmed, calmed traffic area, London XXL, what makes these habitants trust signs like prophecies, The Mad Hatter Hotel, Alice's head emerging from an exquisite corpse, the uncertainty of the poet in a headless bust next to cut bananas, the small squiggles of Miro finding her wherever she is, this is a kind of attraction when the vast sheets of rust stand in corners and a girl in black regards the jackdaw and the crow pierced through their hearts on a very white wall and the idea of two walls meeting is not terrifying any longer. Red polka dot spheres hang in a galaxy of people, on the screen the red wig is synonymous with sanity, she lives in a mental asylum and makes her art, seeing dots everywhere, holes in her vision, holes like punch-holes, leaving paper-dots like a Hansel trail across forests of rubble. Bourgeois not a class but a name, photomontage makes skeletons possible, and butter, the only way to read a newspaper is to wrap it around the eyes, driving bullets into a flat iron is a way of making conversation in a very dead room, small printed books appeal like little children, their guile is practised, they are small and cry out to be picked up and held, even put in pockets close to the heart. Shelley reigns over lamb's shank and ale, even in the middle of a great river a big barge can assert stillness, crowds inherit airlessness, old powerhouses are determinedly ugly so they can startle you with loveliness within, or violence, or calculated gentility, no one dares be flashy here and voices are lowered slowly like wheelchair lifts while in another room the very soft sound of splashing is not a distant memory but a very near one, near understood as intimate, logic tipping its front wheel into the air so it can get off the train without bumping its precious cargo. It felt shabby, he said, holding his clear bright opinions in the palm of a forgotten hand. Perhaps no cloud can come between two people built this small. What was beautiful continues to be beautiful in a house with a bright yellow door.

Never before has Space Gulliver dreamed
Rather never before been conscious on waking
That what she had was a dream
In another country that felt like hers
She saw herself in a changing booth
A flimsy contraption of wood with a sliver of mirror
Nailed to the door
Open to the elements
Which included sun and a light breeze
And the voices of two men
Who
        Peering out, clutching
        A top to her chest, half-dressed
She sees are busy at work
Inside a pillar of stone:
One sets out his equipment, knives, plates,
Nuts, he is a betel-nut-cutter
She knows it though she has never seen one before
The other is on his phone
Chattering his spiel
He is a broker and she is filled with admiration
At their ability to work
To make a living
To make the most of what could be no more than a landing
In a building with little light
Or a disused mall
With an atrium full of shadows
And an unwashed glass roof
So when you look up
It's always afternoon

On a day the world will end
    If they look up they will see her
Trying on clothes made of the lightest cotton
Yellow green lightly patterned falling softly against her skin
A sheerness that makes her aware of the limitations
Of the clothes she has been wearing
That feel like pillars around her legs
Shields around her chest
Another kind of spacesuit
In which the air must never enter
For it's the air that could kill her
Freeze her
Make her sick with frost
        On waking
Space Gulliver is filled with longing for clothes
That slip away
Flutter sing
Small soft buttons no zippers anywhere necks deep waists
    flared
A gentleness she has not found
In the shirts that hug her body now
Keeping out the cold
One whole hour of her day
Lost to the falsity of clocks

Space Gulliver cannot understand the clocks
If it is already afternoon before she discovers they have been
changed
What does it say of the deception wrought upon her
As she slowly waltzed her way through morning
Believing an extra hour to be the ground
On which her feet were moving
What does it say of time
The table she sits at every morning
Like a true denizen
Picking up the fork and spoon of minute and hour
To eat the day
Nourish herself
This appetizing meat
This garden-fresh leek
These potatoes straight from the ground
Which now
It seems is no more
Than a raft
A square of enchanted rug
Pulled away
So suddenly
Space Gulliver refuses seconds
She is hungry yes
But one hour has gone down the drain
Like trash
And everyone calm in the conspiracy
Of loss
Discussing Sunday like a traffic update
Unemotional
If only she had known!

She would have saved that hour
Moment by moment
O
Penning each wistful dying instant
Sketch with two fingers
In the box within a box within a box
The purple beaded round box with the pieces of mirror
Inside its velvet lining
This hour like a jewel
A pin
An earring
An elephant
That she might gift
To the girl who needs it most
The girl who did not seize the extra day
When she could have asked and won her man
What would she not give for the extra hour
Space Gulliver is hatching for her!
She waits for the eggs to boil.
I am good with eggs.
A good egg.
The best egg I ever ate.
Unembarrassed by her eulogy to eggs
Space Gulliver waits for them to reach the hardness
She is accustomed to
If she had boiled them yesterday during the lost hour
Believing herself still tied to earth
Perhaps she might have
Found they weren't farm-fresh free-range after all
But ancient
The primordial Egg
From which Brahma arose from his sleep

And Marici from his eye
And all the aeons
Of inhuman godly time
Which the clocks around her
Cannot comprehend
Encompass
Imagine
Leave alone
Measure
I might change my name yet
          Space Gulliver grins
To Continuum

When the great shadow moves into Space Gulliver's heart
Turquoise purple verdigris coats its skin
Flecks of blue
Suck out her life as she wonders
Blood, why blood
Bloody
What wars were lost on this land where sheep dwell
And blue shoes dig into soft deep sand
Each rock a ravaged face
No sense in wading from cove to cove
Handcuffs to headphones
Where will she walk to next time
With her pockets full
Of stones?
Age shall not wither her
As she watches the flock
Paint their fingernails orange and hang
Feathers
From their ears
Beautiful birds with nests they are not afraid
To leave
Gorse lights up the landscape leaden in the cold
        Somewhere
Space Gulliver knows
        There must be another way out

TAKE COURAGE the white brick advises above the awful symmetry of brown houses linked to each other like flesh that cannot be separated operated upon a deathly congealing. What slides sideways interests the eye that refuses to admit the vacancy of the landscape trying to fill it, the hypnosis of mechanical voices monotoning the non-lullaby where coaches and the separation of trains advise take courage be sure you are in the right seven of seven front and rear everything must be discouraged as you look sideways at the little street under Borough Market, a wilful nonchalance, if his hands could sketch this too, she would put it in a little book that would open at the touch of a moist finger. Hither Green, a sylvan tempting, being soothed may not be surrender, show some Pluckley, toss a Head of Corn, London Bridge isn't falling down, we don't live in Knightsbridge anymore, names were songs before they were places trodden under her foot stumbled over rambled around and tossed away. Growltiger the tabby cat, Black Lion with very green eyes poised on a stump, striped grey portrait of Feline in Fenêtre. The howling of foxes, amorous he says, territorial she says, ugly and sad, they both say, a tearing to pieces antagonism. Swans expect to be fed. On the riverbank, bodies shaped by wind and water carry long and narrow boats upon their heads, haunches moving in perfect symmetry. Cities race down the river, high tide rising, is that a giant grey snail half-sunk in the mud, no, a metal grey chair flung overboard Little Jim, everything must be named, Victory, but what of the cracks on the pavement the little yellow locks on black posts the possibility of opening your front door and finding the steps awash in river, what of the small puffs of smoke from the chimney, proof of habitation, of fire? The boat people are best. She reads each book with a slow intensity, unravels questions that must be asked and answered in the surefooted manner of walkers accustomed to bridges and tracks overhead accustomed to islands square patches of censorious garden accustomed to the fickleness of light the feather worecast the parrot keeler the bumbling of letters from beginning to end.

The last time Space Gulliver looked
The pewter pitcher was at the bottom of the sea and
The griffin in the sky was
Swallowing the
Tale of the serpent
A harp was playing as if
Without
The aid of human hands and
As the rainbow
Arched its back from one
Side of the lough to
The other
The boats broke loose from
The pier
          Inside her
Space Gulliver sensed twenty-four
Strings
Tense like
Whipcord hours
Plucked one by one by a small
Metal object for which plectrum is
Not the right word
From violet to red the eye can
Only see so
Much
Under the skylight
Cloudlight
White as paper
As snow
If one of the plaster angels turned into a polar bear right
Now Space Gulliver would not be

Shocked
If the small wooden desk with brass knobs were
To turn into a galleon
Wrecked by wind and water
        Wood sinks
Men die
Only objects remain
Like the sough of
The sea
        Bowls jugs whisks
        Collars red woollen
        Fragments
        Silk tassle
        Hemp piece
        Wheel with barnacle
        Comb
Imperishable
        Parts of shoes
        Cittern
        Resin
        Weaving heddle
        Wooden heart
Could use a wooden heart meself
Space Gulliver sings to the strum of the
Sleet
Hail stones like
Mary
Against the window
'Used to tighten the rope-stays which helped
To secure the mast'
        Shipwrecked by gales of

Tiredness
Space Gulliver cries
Easily
Flares into small childish
Rages
Feels her cheeks cold from the starlit
Wind
Wishes to drown just
For the lap of
Silk over her head
The move from sea to lough to bay to
Pool to hidden rushing murmur under
                                        The rock
The place where water springs like a blessing into
Her palms
Unpronounce
Each name and
Stay
Speechless
Space Gulliver tells herself in the manner of
Admonition
Stay
Tight
Secure
Across the bay
The prison sits
Random that house
With grass on its roof
Keep looking
        Back
In case you miss
The mermaid and

As you pass the overhanging
Cliff
Believe you are the last person on this
Planet
While on the other side
In that other
Planet of dark and gorse and rock another
Space Gulliver draws
Down the mist
Prepares for unseen landings
Withdraws from comprehension

Stella my unspeaking companion at the trestle table, refreshing and cold, the way she knows to be on a day that feels like summer. A lad on the loose, footing his own bill, staring at the girls who pass by with blind and angry glare. Unwashed hair intermingles. There is a baldness to this dexterity with books slung across narrow shoulders. Stella presses her cold cheek against mine, encourages the sending of messages about meetings that will never come to pass. What you want too much won't happen, what you barely imagine will. A small room, a bed, perhaps this is a largesse she can extend. Finding your way in a library is like learning Braille, your fingers need to see, height is an asset, just as friendly assistance. The inside of rooms cloying with heat, pressing temples, each layer too much, strip down, away. Even strangeness loses its strangeness after a while, cathedral ignored, sun bathed in, grass lain on, it takes sheer will to maintain the distance between you and unmeant invites. How much do you want to earn, do you have a girlfriend? Russian dolls, mushroom pirogi, free jazz in the foyer, Stella, shall we go home?

Sometimes hunger is only thirst, Space Gulliver
Tells the girl who is ravenous again
Think inter-galactic drip-dry
Think big freeze
King penguin
Anything to take your mind off the last sausage
A poem in a bus by a fourteen year old
Lusting after the party sausage that a dog filches
From under her nose
          At that very minute a dog enters the bus
Grey-haired and slightly blind
Like his owner
Wotchamacallit is whistling again
Whatsit is standing on tiptoe eating crackers and cheese
The golden sheep on her mantelpiece is happy to be back
Unlike her who is fickle and treacherous
And wants to fill emptiness with noise
Like another kind of eating

As beautiful as the bottom of a bowl of porridge, he said, looking at the fog. But she meant it, it was beautiful, and she had not yet understood suffocation to be the element, standing outside the locked hard door of a difficult poetry discussed in a small heated room with chairs that sink you. Listening can be productive, sitting among strangers, thinking, not saying what crosses your mind because first you must test it out, alone. The tall black man in fire-engine red, the little almond girl with the matchless voice. 'Stand awhile and ponder on man's intolerance to man.' Meanwhile the plum blossoms or are they cherry fall around her, the crocuses are open, daffodils everywhere, shocking how tall they are since she saw them last, Humpty Dumpty sat in a meadow, in the Old Weaver's House you must mind your step, your head, visors leak light onto your table, crossed spears everywhere, a Spitfire explodes bitter on your tongue while the lady behind you with her accent slipping away confuses cider for bitter, bitter lemon, the German waiter keeps repeating, bitter lemon. There is a garden of tables outside but she has chosen to sit below the street in an alcove snug with light and wood and regard the faces that pass through her like a storm. Two old men who could be lovers, the soothing sound of French, the American ordering pizza talking too loud, 'I like that little bite', three kinds of roast lamb, the guy with the glares, the girl with the headscarf, armour, amour, here they come the hordes! She lives here now, that frees her from having to see sights, rivers, museums, she can see them any time or not at all, what matters is knowing that Black Griffin Lane is congenial, the Hot Sausage Co. perennial, Falstaff and Marlowe the names of pubs you can order steak and kidney pie at, and somewhere a downstairs with low chairs and Moroccan food. This is also a postcard, says the old man, minding his head and his step, stepping in.

Space Gulliver can breathe again
The kind of breathing that rides the sun on its back
Watches steam rising into mouths
Is aware of the changeness of sound
The way wheel on tar can meld into
The ceaseless breathing of the road
For months now a patch of land had glittered into her existence
So sharp it could only be sheet metal, water or mercury
This morning in its exact location
A patch of yellow like a piece of mirror flashing the sun
Rape seed
The ugly word flowering into the approximation of mustard
The light of home
        They never taught them to breathe
        There were machines that did that
        For them
Space Gulliver could hold that
Against them
Against herself
Who took her away
        The slowness of it flabbergasts her
For days she buckled under
Over-oxygenation of lungs
It was specially keen on heights, shores
The wind that represented distance, very great distance
And complete absence of suspended particulate matter
The daily infliction that she breathed in readiness
For a life closer to the hub, where empty space existed
Only to be filled
By building, tower, bridge, not gaze, water, tree
        Her breath taken away

And in its place the dragon of delight
Scaled all over
Red and glittering with exhaustion
Tasmania, she felt like saying to the island before her
Mozambique
Instead ethereal names and bays that sank around her
And the tiredness of holding the dragon where no one could
See
Its redness entering her eyes
Its scales her tongue
Until every night she had to fight to sleep the way she liked
Curled up on her side
Every talon breaking
Into an ache no sword could kill
Brace, bracing, braced
Feeling in her shoulders a readiness to battle
Pointed wings emerging
That would eat the miles between place and place
Space Gulliver took flight in reversal
Back to bed
Sleep
Family not hers but warm and alien enough
To feel like
Home
That word she has used twice in one morning without loss
Or love or longing
Just the sense of its preparedness
Its waitingness
The patience of rooms
That she would give anything to learn
But not just yet, not when she has finally learnt
How to breathe again and her body flesh again

And her heart unbroken
        It took her twenty-one days
Forgive me, dragon, she says with new tenderness
It wasn't you that hurt me
I can ride you now
Alone
Here, let me breathe for you
Steam in your mouth
Salve in your wound
The sword I must now remove from your side

In shocking black wetsuit the angler by the canal, bitter weather no deterrence to his grim reaper stance, head zipped into black mask, rod barely moving. When the students leave, the rabbits return, the poet had said to her. There he is, the brown rabbit, hunkered down in the grass in posture reminiscent of hatching eggs or meditation. Behind him, the lost gull walking like a pedant in the disabled car park. Out of dug holes houses rise. Left the map behind and now she must ask strangers, not one aware which street they walk on, where they live, which turn will lead to the Foundry where the beer is pumped frothing into the mouths of stout brown bottles, will lead to the closed-face of the building with the secret fire-escape like breaking and entering a home. Walk down Hawk Lane. Preserve the password for later. At tables for four and six, dandelion coffee and crimson silk shirts, what is it like, Bombay? Each time, the answer swerves around her, a car that might flip over with no warning, leaving the driver to crawl out, intact, unaware of the child's great fear in the car that narrowly missed collision. Sometimes, she hears herself saying, it's like a nightmare worth having, and then, does it matter to you if the poems aren't read in sequence? Accretion matters, describe the city spatially, Rome not Bombay, architecture as constructing space. The artist with Mac-light on his face plays the sounds of south London, reminding her of a Bombay she invents on the spot, warehouse doors opening, winches, machinery, drones, two robots making love, short circuiting as they touch, it doesn't feel mechanical, she stares at the sound as if it were image, in her head the lightness that brings her back to earth. Scarves unwind, rewind like conversation. In the Black Forest, there is no undergrowth. No light reaches the ground.

Place has encroached her, Space Gulliver no longer
Able to *wish nothing but the best for you*
Resist the specificity, the voice of an English singer
Crooning her sentimental words masquerading at bitter-
Sweet truths for those who care not to think too hard
No longer able to erase the place names one by one
So that when asked where she has been all these days
She could say with the honesty of a born liar
Nowhere
Trieste
Tristesse
Owhere
The old word for 'some place'
The sum of all the places
She has seen with the blindness of the obsessive traveller
So that when five coloured rings are raised in a green park
Below a baroque clock
She resents being so close to the future
The imminent that she wishes to avoid like the big event
Millions will come to see and only a few hundred flee from
'South Bank' she wants to say ripping it from the grey walk
Along any river not this one
Take without knowledge
Like translating a foreign tongue
Not being a mind-reader
Rip them from tradition
Poems like flowers blooming inwards
Invented characters drawn on little pieces of card
Poetry like lightning
Reduce the number of dangerous dogs

The backstreet breeding
Swapped for playstations
Armies of danger
The boy who died in his flat was unhappy living in London
Who wouldn't be, Space Gulliver thinks
If only she knew what to do with this nearness
That might have been alluring if it had been unavailable
Disinterest in old ruins could be seen as a handicap
Just as disinclination to pore over beautiful things
In an overheated building filled with the loot of empires
She would rather breathe the sleet, the rain
Swallow the air
Dis
Diss
Dissect
Her indifference to the noble and ennobling
Give me, Space Gulliver thinks, a shaky too-tall bar-stool
And many listeners, the smell of new pages cut with hesitation
The face of the boy who sits quietly waiting to draw
The next pint

The Lazarus Requiem through the grey sky in a shaft of light, Handel's death, Handel's gate, white façade urban legend of the Messiah in Dublin, 'this proud and arrogant city moves secretly in my blood', censored, re-introduced, the line in the poet's writing all over the white margins, 'balls in my fist, impotent worm on my thigh'. Malachite the colour of the duck's neck, the feathers glinting blue and green. That morning she dreamt a sky 'shattered by stars'. Do you remember everything, he had asked, a summer ago. Yes, she had said, that word now seen as a lie. Only the embedded chips on the wall, the witch, the broomstick, the omagh, the ladder. Only the sound that came from Merchant's Arch, music for the streets, the locks intertwined on Halfpenny Bridge. The little typewriter that Synge wrote on, small enough to hurl out of a window. 'He said' shown as a lion's paw. The colours orange and purple, Armenian, Ethiopian. Belfast everywhere as she leaves and enters Dublin. The Liffey seen at all tides and times, each clock unreliable. 'Four good ghazals', the stress in the wrong place. Ulysses, the unreadable icon. Old man carefully smoothing sand into a sand dog. Longbow behind bars. Freezing in the House of the Dead. Knowledge of loss, days lost, and nothing to show for it but broken boots, and a hole where the world should have been.

Where is the constellation, the drone of the voice in
        Space Gulliver's ears
Claiming resurrected stars as alter-egos
Contemporary blues afflicting the women around her
Like a virulent brand of music
The dial turning from hiss to hiss
The unbearable guttering of voices barely able to cohere
Around sentences
These people's
Insouciant ignorance
        Next morning when the day is thrown into disarray
        By the danger
She had yearned for
The siren shrieking about her head
Everyone out in their pajamas
Space Gulliver realizes with a new shame
That she too was caught unprepared
        She of a previous state
        Of readiness
In a moment of insouciance
That doesn't sit well on her
Who has never been able to shrug off even the slightest loss
        Claiming every mistake as hers
All the guilt in the universe
On her fanatical shoulders
She rushes bareheaded barefoot into the cold car park
And discovers what she really needs to live is
Not what she imagined
Neither water nor clothes nor chocolate
But machines recording her
Money preserving her

Paper creating her
Anxiety destroying her
        Back inside, she sniffs the air for burning
And cooks lunch

Space Gulliver remembers the story being told:
Town Mouse and Country Mouse
Both are her
And when she is one she loathes the other
Wishes like her friend
That she had been a horse
Even a cold mare in a thick red rug of a blanket
If not a stallion silhouetted against the sky
Wonders if she wishes
That precisely
Or is osmotic again
Reciting
If wishes were horses then
                If *its* and *ans* were
                                I'd have
                                Plenty
Scraps
The only kind of nourishment
She can give and take
Simultaneously

Space Gulliver on a bus, that creature, comfort
Known to her from the toes up
At twelve minutes past the hour
She will be warned again
        To sit, the greatest luxury
        Regard pools the width of roads
Things move inside her eyes
        Re-guard the loon
To be the only
Inhabitant, had she not wished for just
Such a monstrosity
Bird calls
Solitary runner
Double-decker gladness at being the sole reason
The earth orchestrated to her whims
Baby buggies must give up
To wheelchairs
Invalid note of caution
When thought was wrenched away
Replaced by
Scenes
That was when
The trouble began
Moving things inside her eyes
Empress of the vehicle un-
Obstructed by talk
SLOW DOWN
The road tells her as she lazes
The curve that will hasten the city
Towards her
All the other faces

Those whose home-
Coming must happen just once a year
The Chinese characters
A frieze of sound
Comforting because foreign
GIVE WAY
To the last announcement
PUSH TO OPEN
New routes
Have hatched
So comfortably

How many
Ways
Can you
Approach
The same
Cathedral
How many kinds
Of light
Can change
What you thought you
Knew

Wandering down a river watching ducks is what the sunshine makes her do, forget errands, prefer meandering, the penultimate destination, the one you weren't supposed to go to. How does the tall punter duck under the low bridge, how slow must his drift be for walkers to outpace it? You are not vulnerable, he says, as they drive into the dark. But I am, she wants to say, vulnerable to every body that rests against mine, vulnerable to the word 'eagle', to the shape of shoes, fallen arches, raised insteps, the idea of the scar that the knife has left around the heart, saving it with a tiny metal insertion.

This addiction to the shelf is bad, Space Gulliver get a
move on
Peer over the rim of oranges and apples
Stop mistaking bananaglow for sunshine
That's a pear not a passerby
Sponge cake
Absorbent mind
Recall temperatures
Like submarines
Plunged below
The body will heal itself like a great blue ribbon

And so the soft wet rain of the bandaged hand
The ship aground
Like green sprouting at the knees
The wind-chaser
Like the sock in an aerodrome
Hello
She says to the spires
I'm back

It's only rain when you can hear it, Space Gulliver says
Pounding pelting skittering spattering
Drumming
Oh the sheer drama of it!
This soft falling is a nothing
A lulling
A failure of feeling
Softness that betrays
An endless misery
An empty soup

It's only wind when you can see it

Waving
Ruffling
Breaking the hearts of trees into striations of utter beauty
Tossing trampolines ten feet into the air
Smashing roofs
Baring the foolishness of roads
That know nothing of how to deal with a tree that has
Wrenched its roots and fallen
Into glass hedge or fence
Toppled like a helpless giant
Revealing enormous chunks of earth
Cracking tar into the thin pretence it is

But all that at the lower level where towns still exist

Full of exits and roundabouts
Here on this vantage point, nothing but grass and clarity
The wind singing
Of speed and silence
Not incompatible
Singing of the labyrinth
The shaman

The sapling with coloured ribbons tied around it
Memorial to a twenty-one year old boy
The black and white dog, not Dalmatian
        Blowing hair
        Frosted lips
        Chimera
        Sanctuary
        Bedevilment
        The whole planet spinning around her
And she steady
The one
The fiercest wind cannot uproot toss or fell
As if all her prior movement was apprenticeship
To immobility
Racing like the wind
Not her story anymore
But the wind's

Three windmills like apparitions at the end of the longest village in Wales. A horse with a windblown mane and an intelligent face as if he would speak. The white wolf-dog in the Abbey among the graves, tall as a house. The slow naming of places, Stream of Blue Water, Head of the Estuary, Belly of the Sun. The light ship with red sides, the black and white Norwegian once-was-a-church spilling with people, exhibits A B and C. The mood-ring turns to purple, no correspondence on the chart. At the mouth of river after river a desire to drink deep. The water's high, she says, and imagines the drunken bliss of water intoxicated by sun, drinking too much too quickly, swallowing towns and intelligent horses, burial chambers and cairns, peace meetings and three sets of flags sun-roofs sandwiches horseshoes and luster jugs, the slanting pillars of a house designed by an alcoholic, he says in jest, painted white thick walls of the coach-house where they sleep in vivid extensions of light. Strumblehead, Fishguard, Fair of the Heath, Village of the Poets, iron age dwelling in which a tall woman may stand upright in a belly of stone, looking out at the sea, scrambling rocks like morse, our word for gorse is 'eithin', we see the flowers, they see the thorns. A sad maiden, a midden, a conjured war, the noise of Anglesey, Tiger Bay, White Hart, red white and black lions everywhere, the animal foreign fierce and farthest from them, majestic, and male. Three butchers in one town, a medicine hall, mayors in golden chains, choirs in carmine jackets feeding their faces untuneful. Cross Hands, the sign says. Truly cross hands, angry, fretful, even perhaps raging Under Milkwood in a cluster of huts, from the sea blue Moby Dick rises, call me Ishmael the poem began, a too-handsome man playing Ahab like a rock. The voice of the

Ancient Mariner was born here, he who read the poem into her young and feckless heart, smiting her with story. A little houseboat named Porthos missing Aramis and Athos, the harbour where Scott sailed from, the harbour where Amelia landed with coal on her face blinked at by Dai Harvey unable to say Porth Tywyn, Gateway to the Sands, hiding from the press of people and news and in the sky this minute the two planes, circling, flying low, as if looking, like her, for signs.

Space Gulliver has been hearing sheep again.
The distinct maaa-aaaa that seemed hallucinatory
And too close to her window far from any sheep field
To be real
        Or was it really a cow?
Space Gulliver's knowledge of animals is notional
As if gained from a picture book
But when it came again, the distinct bleat not moo
She found herself leaning towards it
As if magnetized
        Why: 'as if'
Instead of simply, directly: Gained, Magnetized?
As if!
The curling lip of a sheep hurt at being mistaken for a cow
        Perhaps she is, say it, a secret pastoralist
Space Gulliver: City Chick
A blatant pose
Accumulated from years of severe study
Immersion in fantasies of human occupation
        'Chandler'
        'Ragamuffin'
        'Sewer'
Space Gulliver once met a man who lived for three hundred
        years
In a tunnel under that city she loved most
No one suspected when he emerged
That he was not 'one of ours'
Such were their chameleon powers
She and the others from Elsewhere
                        Whereelse
Perhaps all she wants is to lie gloriously next to the tulips
Count the ducks

Apologize to them for not bearing crumbs
Speak to sky root stone
As if they were her kin
        Shedding metres of skin
        Is only painful for the hot-blooded
All evening a gull spiralled upward
In slowly widening showy circles
While around him in corkscrew wobble
Another less fluent gull
Stuttered on the sharp wind
Never letting the showgull's panache
Faze him as he fluttered like torn paper
Around the maestro
        Where did he learn such equipoise
When did every word-ending tend toward
        'Dhow'?
Tachycardia, Space Gulliver says
        Try that one for size

It is the same sheep that looks at her from the mantelpiece in his golden sleep etched fleece of snow which falls from writing like prescience. The same as the one she described, papier mâché mush of her love too heavy for a helium balloon. The sheep who was a human in the book in a Hokkaido Hotel. The teacosy white and fluffy with black ears and nose this unbelievable cuteness she is falling for like essential precipitation. All *hers* coincide when the body moves from line to line the corrected line the corseted caressed and coerced line. The sheep that left on an overland train chugging slowly through fields where magic might happen to another person with kindness inside her. House of rose rosemary primrose lavender lilac hyacinth cynthia nettle that does not sting ring a ringa roses violets are blue bluebells with curled caps chamomile the unnamed forgotten Latin. House of enchanted robes and fireplace cats growing out of boxes fat cats flipping through cat flaps cat naps on the doorstep, Figaro, shall we dance? Satantango meditango, a well is a point of water what is the point of water if not to ease us away from fixity and the parched eye the split house the violent reconstruction. Remember concrete. Foundation myth only for children who challenge and grow wise as hazel. When the blue candle is lit in its silver holder on the wall the smell of vanilla and honey appears. Teapots can always be broken. That is the comforting fact. And fires lit. When in doubt turn up your collar, dress in your alter-ego, today I will be an elephant, the Dalai Lama, the Renoir family, today my room is Storm Cellar, yours Anathema. It is the crooked gate that will not close that lasts. A hat lasts three years. When the people in the novel lean on you the pressure is pleasant. 'The pressure of the asparagus,' she says as she enters the kitchen. Silence like a clear glass. Not reading like a clearing in a forest of trees. The squirrel creating the tree as he climbs it. Women like watches. One day the sheep will return.

Abandon this 'she', Space Gulliver rages
Bury her in the compost heap
Where her sickening sweetness belongs
All natural things rotting in that precise combination
        'She'
A novel nobody reads anymore
Except a Chinese exile
Drinking empty tea
The calmness that isn't hers but *hers*
Now the need to disentangle
And renew with force
Even violence
Her apartness
Call me it
If that would save me from being the 'she'
That speaks to toads
        Single out the fresh cut
On a slab
And buy it
Devour with a terrible greed
Perhaps that fish that cold fish
Will take away this soft belly
Cowardice
The war of dice
Every word portmanteau
        What she really needs is a ship to sail away in
Leaving 'her' behind
To grow worms

Everything is mine, she says, who need no longer be named
To the plump woodchuck and its mirror-mate
Though my preference is always the street
The word 'seed' need not be agrarian
Do you understand
Its flammability
A ruse under 'the unemotional tongue'
Algiers...
        And then?
Signification
        Every crowd a hymnal
        If you let it out
Beyond the red door
Rooms with Zimbabwe on the walls

The cheap nostalgia of songs she might have
Grown up with if she
Hadn't been so impatient
And so far away in a foreign
Land

concentration

harmony

shock

This is how

A bridge is made

Wrench

(elbow)

By wrench

(heart)

'Walking on the moon' in a mechanical voice
Large moon-faced table of pale wood

If occupied solitarily

Kitchen
The place of perfection
Sea of Tranquility
Heath and heather

Tip of tongue on white porcelain
Like cat drinking milk

Radio waves

pleasure

In the Skin of a Lion

Ski socks not out of place

When fingers need thawing
Against the cup

Runneth over

Archaic and apt
As the cars enter the branches she sees butterflies on speed
That was her flaw
Not to be able to croon
To use throatily
Her entire flotilla of longing
Set sail
        Village of small rain

When the circle is inhabited, she loses her love
For this corner of the world where
Perimeters shift
Slipping past forty acres
To blue houses
With every flower but rose in their nameable gardens
Because Rose is indoors
Brewing tea in an orange pot
Daughter, Rose, wood rose
Stolen to present to a teacher
Tuberose, Rosasharn
          Space Gulliver's interest in flowers
Is the Little Prince's
Lost lover on a small planet
Gallant with shade and water
Tilting into
          Accidental swans
Small steps sideways
Round dance
In a square
Near the stream
          Where gypsies live like dandelions

Raggedness of tapes in a day of jonquils, word from a distant story. Ceilings low enough to touch. Brown rabbit running away, every dappled page a meadow: will be missed, will miss, unforeseen.

In The Year of the Cat Space Gulliver
Who has accepted again her false and barefaced Name
Was five
Hot coals frightened her
Woodsheds
The nightmare of a bear
Snails
Because their slime
Seemed unmentionable

Shrapnel sound striking skin headless shadow on the ceiling drumming mermaids into tunnels white light on her face the maker of image. Outside where trout is eaten the trains pass empty at this time of night. The city is coming alive. Leaving thickens like lead. Music in alleyways never found until now. Shake the hand earn the right to laziness argue the percentage of road deaths wish you had spoken to one person at a time like he was the last the only person. When she runs across the car park in the rain the sheep with illness in its legs a camera in its eyes turns its head towards her the animal possessed by artificial god, the animal placed as offering, the animal that is not animal at all but machine, benign or malign, sick beast regarding her through thinning rain. Mackerel pickled in vinegar, the circumstantial evidence of trout, the blind place in Madrid where canes walk, a long thin policeman who cautions about fog lights. Westgate the beginning of orientation, the blinking street lamps have a name, a map without scale all she ever knew, long windows in the Old Synagogue and wooden benches in the sudden sun, this, too, happens when a flock of poets crosses the road, pied piper, beware the moon, the Dolphin sings the Book of Hours in a gentle voice, Doom Bar, Golden Braid, neck the beer and leave, this is bonhomie, a high wall with spikes on it, a face that has thinned, eyes large, white forearms, arms not exposed to sun, everything worth remembering will be forgotten, sonnets, found text, lissom like leaves. Apple blossoms fall around her like snow, skyward where her love moves across the grey and open sorrow.

When Space Gulliver finds the sparrow in her room
Beating its wings against the window she has left wide open
The terror of her alien presence making it forget the way
It entered
She knows the next visitant is
Ready
          She clears out slowly
Thinking of the way the vacancy she leaves behind
Will be filled again to bursting
Detritus building
A nest that feels safe in the strongest wind
In lack of sun
And how she had arrived with empty hands
And waited for the earth to turn

ACKNOWLEDGEMENTS

This book would never have been written without the Charles Wallace India Trust (CWIT) Creative Writing Fellowship 2012 which gave me a three-month residency at the University of Kent, Canterbury (UKC). For the award and the opportunity, I wish to thank Richard Alford of the CWIT and Alex Padamsee of UKC. For your fabulous recommendations which played no small role in my getting the Fellowship, thank you, Mani Rao and Arundhathi Subramaniam.

At the university, I'd like to thank Peter Brown and the English department for their many kindnesses with time, office space and administrative help. Thank you, Alex Padamsee, among all the other things, for books lent and hospitalities received, and Lyn Innes, for making me feel special in so many big and little ways. Patricia Debney, for the warmth and wisdom of your presence and poetry, the affection and energy with which you made me feel part of the Kent poetry community. Jan Montefiore, for the wonderful experience of exchanging and talking about our poems, for blue-bell sightings, culinary delights, and the pleasure of getting to know Patrick and Henry (and their writing). Caroline Rooney, for an unforgettable evening of food, wine and camaraderie. Simon Smith, for lucid insights into translation, salaam! Nancy Gaffield, for your gentle spirit and your luminous poems. Sarah Wood, for the depth, intensity and clarity of your thinking and writing, and for your friendship. David Herd, for the conversations about poetry and process, for drawing me into the spirit of the Zone, for the power of your poetry and for the extraordinary gift of having read and responded with such generosity to this book while it was still in manuscript form — to each of you, my gratitude is profound.

The students, whose paths briefly crossed mine via workshops and readings, whose poems touched and impressed me, I shall always remember with fondness.

Thanks beyond measure to Pauline McGonagle and Richard Hooton whose home and hearts were always open during my stay in Kent. Without your sane advice, your practical help and the sheer joy of your company, I'd have been truly lost. And Olga Efimova, thanks for being such a fabulous flatmate!

To my dear friends, old and new, in England, Wales and Ireland – Rasna Dhillon, Eric Jacobson, Aarti Shah, Tobie Munthe, Edel Pyrgos, Imelda McGuinness, the McGuinness, McGonagle, McCourt, Doherty and Bonner families, Martin and Mererid Hopwood, Alaw and Hywel Griffiths, Karen Owen, Alexandra Büchler, Gerður Kristný, Sioned Puw Rowlands, Siân Melangell Dafydd, Eurig Salisbury, Twm Morys, Jan Morris, Bill Herbert, Brian Holton and the ever-generous Todd Swift – thank you for making my visit and my life so multitudinously rich. The news of Professor Jon Stallworthy's passing away in 2014 makes the memory of an afternoon of tea and conversation in his Oxford office in 2012 all the more precious.

To Kiran David, beloved friend and husband, who bore my long absence with characteristic patience, I dedicate this book. To Ma and Baba, my love, always.

To my dear publishers and editors, V.K. Karthika and Shantanu Ray Chaudhuri, my grateful thanks for continued faith; to the team at HarperCollins, thanks for taking care of everything; to Rajinder Ganju, thanks for elegant and meticulous typesetting; and finally, to Prasanna Sankhé, for the cover, muchas gracias!

Judith Albert, thank you for making the art that inspired my first Space Gulliver poems http://www.journalfuerkunstsexundmathematik.ch/2010/01/14/judith-albert-19/ and Nils Röller, Barbara Ellmerer and Yves Netzhammer, thanks for making space on your wonderful Journal for Art, Sex and Mathematics for the poems, which I append as a Postscript for those who are curious about where Space Gulliver returned *from*...

While on the other side
In that other
Planet of dark and gorse and rock another
Space Gulliver draws
Down the mist
Prepares for unseen landings

Space Gulliver

Pinned to the ground that is her shadow
By a thousand Lilliputian laughs.

Nothing can touch her.

Sing a melody that will untangle
The dark cloud of her hair.

Is this the box they will bury me in?
Her day has been rigid, and square.

Neither bone nor blood.

What she longs for is
The heart of a helium circle.

She sees patterns everywhere.

Space Gulliver II

Space Gulliver is dreaming of an egg.
She believes she has cracked the conundrum of the egg.

Yellow matters, she hears a voice in the dream whisper
in her ear, there where the strings sing. What matters

is keeping the yellow intact. She listens harder.
Space Gulliver is dreaming of the void.

No, the voice whispers in the shell of her ear, the ovoid.
That is what you're dreaming of, the shape

of enclosure and escape, you even wrote a poem about it
once, remember? Space Gulliver has forgotten.

Oblivion is the mirror that hides a cave. Listen, the voice
whispers in her pale pink ear, is that the sea?

Space Gulliver III

'Food'. 'Pickle'. 'Chalk'. For some reason that
can be attributed to hunger of various kinds, maybe,

Space Gulliver finds these words floating before her.
She isn't sure where they came from, whether their arrival

will be followed by the real things, food, pickle, and chalk.
She could use a little food, something to see her through

another night. She always liked picking out the garlic
from the pickle. Now, in a yahooland where no one

has heard of the Bermuda Triangle, she feels all tastes
are disappearing. Bitter gourd, sweet lime, sour plantain.

Variables, constants. Space Gulliver is looking for a line,
a chalk mountain, a little white sign on a black, black slate

Space Gulliver IV

'A parallelogram is a telegram from a parallel world,'
a being in a red hat says, taking out a little notebook.

'Let me give you my coordinates.' And instead of latitude
and longitude, as Space Gulliver expects, the being,

whose hat is now an obscure shade of ochre, reels off
a series of sounds like horses neighing, like vowels

and consonants, like numbers from a nightmare.
'Whether you find me is immaterial,' the being says,

sounding like himself again, in other words, sounding
like wind in the trees, snow on the grass, willows weeping

into water. 'It's the Houyhnhnm that counts.'
There are many beings here, roaming the ether.

Are they real? Is that a parking meter? A lamp post?
Is this what it means, to travel?

Space Gulliver V

This poem exists only as an audio file: to hear it, please visit: http://www.journalfuerkunstsexundmathematik.ch/2010/02/23/sampurna-chattarji-space-gulliver-v/

Space Gulliver VI

Thank you, she said, for the trance, elation.
For the click click click of words falling into place.
For the clack clack clack of the knitting loom.

Breath is a silver fog. Birds build palaces.
Cross the lake. Join the jungle.

I see it!
Is that not what you said?
Let me try again. There was a city I left behind.
It drowned in rain.

Insect girls lived in jars, buildings walked on stilts.
The name had a bomb in it, had a mum in it.
Had a bay in it, had a bye in it...

Does that ring a bell? No?
Fragments of a word.
Brob. Ding. Nag.
I beg your pardon? How many languages do I speak?
Two, she said, pointing to her eyes
and her heart. Just two. And you?

'Why language? They
ask, why not medicine
or magic? Why not
something more useful?'
(Kala Krishnan Ramesh)

The editors at HarperCollins believe that poetry is medicine, magic and more. Committed to publishing the most exciting contemporary poetry from India and the subcontinent, we wanted to celebrate ten of our favourite books by publishing them as special keepsake editions under the 'Poetry 10' series. From sci-fi verse to modern bhakti poetry, long narrative sequences about birth and identity to brief sonnets, each book will speak to lovers (and haters) of poetry with wit, wisdom, clarity and abandon.

3 Sections by Vijay Seshadri
All One's Blue by Kazim Ali
Bearings by Karthika Naïr
Countries of the Body by Tishani Doshi
He Is Honey, Salt and the Most Perfect Grammar by Kala Krishnan Ramesh
Life & Times of Mr S by Vivek Narayanan
Malabar Mind by Anita Nair
Space Gulliver: Chronicles of an Alien by Sampurna Chattarji
Triage: Casualties of Love and Sex by Margaret Mascarenhas
When God Is a Traveller by Arundhathi Subramaniam

In *Space Gulliver*, Sampurna Chattarji chronicles not only the journey of its alien protagonist, but also how one wor(l)d changes into another through cerebral associations. As Space Gulliver careens through various time-frames and tries to take stock of earthly and unearthly objects, the cathedral that is the sky changes its form continually, at times disappearing altogether. The nature of poetry in this collection too is in constant flux and full of fury, absorbing eclectic modes and moods, which may come from the protagonist's encounters with poets, travelling centaurs, a manual for Tibetan grammar and a Dalmatian.

A fantastically engineered sequence, here is poetry that is not afraid to be whimsical and astute at the same time so that in the end, like Space Gulliver, the readers too will be 'no longer terrified of vastness'.